The
HEAVYWEIGHT
CHAMPIONSHIP

Published by Creative Education, Inc.

123 South Broad Street, Mankato, MN 56001

Designed by Rita Marshall with the help of Thomas Lawton

Cover illustration by Rob Day, Lance Hidy Associates

Copyright © 1993 by Creative Education, Inc.

Photography by Allsport, Bettmann Archive, Duomo, Focus on Sports, FPG International, Sports Illustrated (Neil Leifer, Tony Triolo), Wide World Photos

Printed in the United States

Library of Congress Cataloging-in-Publication Data

Ryan, Pat.

The heavyweight championship / Pat Ryan.

Summary: Describes significant moments in the history of the heavyweight boxing championship.

ISBN 0-88682-554-7

1. Boxing—History—Juvenile literature.   2. Boxers (Sports)—Biography—Juvenile literature.   [1. Boxing—History.]   I. Title.

GV1136.R93   1992

796.8'3—dc20

92-7134

CIP

AC

The HEAVYWEIGHT CHAMPIONSHIP

PAT RYAN

CREATIVE EDUCATION INC.

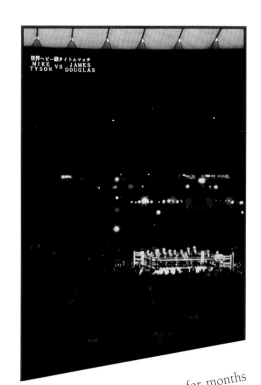

世界ヘビー級タイトルマッチ
MIKE VS JAMES
TYSON DOUGLAS

Boxing fans had been waiting for months for this day. Tickets, which were selling for over one hundred dollars a seat, had been sold out for weeks. Now, with the event still more than three hours away, there was not an empty seat in the stadium.

A sense of excitement was in the air, a feeling that something unexpected might occur. Korakuen Stadium in Tokyo, Japan, was the site of a bout between "Iron Mike" Tyson and James "Buster" Douglas. At stake was the 1990 heavyweight championship of the world.

After seven rounds of the fight, it appeared that the unexpected was happening. The challenger seemed to be winning the match. "Buster, he's yours, you've got him kid," yelled Douglas's trainer. As the eighth round began, the trend continued. Douglas's hand speed was keeping the champion confused. Buster snapped a left to the jaw of the champion, and Tyson's knees trembled. The crowd yelled, sensing an upset.

Douglas (left) versus Tyson.

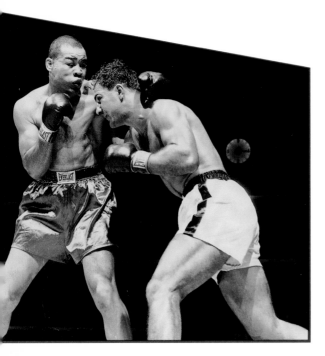

GREAT MOMENTS

From the age of bare-knuckle boxing to the present, the heavyweight championship has produced many great moments. The bout between Mike Tyson and James Douglas is just one brief snapshot. Many others flash in the minds of boxing fans everywhere: John L. Sullivan versus Paddy Ryan; James J. Jeffries versus Bob Fitzsimmons; Jersey Joe Walcott versus Ezzard Charles; Ingemar Johansson versus Floyd Patterson. Each one of these contain memories that provide followers of heavyweight boxing with faces and flashes of greatness.

Since John L. Sullivan was acknowledged as boxing's first heavyweight champion in the late 1800s, the sport has been synonymous with excitement. Yet it has also been a platform for controversy.

The nature of the sport calls for judgment. In most cases, three impartial judges are asked to determine the outcome. Win, lose or draw, their decision is final, if not always popular. The knockout, however, eliminates such judgment. When the referee counts a fallen fighter out at ten, there can be no argument. Or can there?

A second later a camera flashed as the challenger lunged with a right cross. This time, however, Douglas missed. In an instant the champion responded with a classic uppercut to Buster's chin. The crowd roared as Douglas fell to the floor. There were only six seconds left in the round, but it appeared Buster's dream of an upset had ended as the referee began his long, slow count to ten: one . . . two . . . three . . . four . . . five . . . six . . .

Joe Louis (left) confronts Rocky Marciano in an epic 1951 bout.

Challenger Buster Douglas (left) battles Mike Tyson for the heavyweight title.

THE LONGEST COUNT

It was September 22, 1927. Two of boxing's greatest heavyweights were scheduled to do battle at Soldier Field in Chicago. It was to be the biggest fight in history, a rematch of the famed Dempsey-Tunney title bout of 1926.

Jack Dempsey in training.

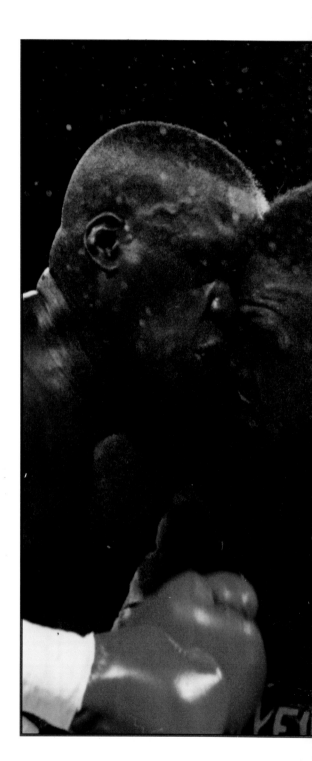

Jack Dempsey, the 1927 challenger.

People gathered from across the country for this great moment in sports. More fans, more journalists, and more money than ever before were expected. Postfight figures would prove this correct. A total of 104,943 spectators paid $2,658,660 to see the spectacle. Most were there to cheer on the challenger, Jack Dempsey. He was the people's champion. His bronzed body and classic good looks had gained Dempsey an enormous following. Now, waiting anxiously like a dog straining at its leash, Jack was ready for the fight to begin.

Two giants collide: Buster Douglas (left) and Evander Holyfield, October 1991.

Dempsey helped popularize heavyweight boxing.

On this night, however, the people's champion was in fact the challenger. Only a year ago Dempsey had been the champion, but a young, unknown fighter by the name of Gene Tunney had changed all that. In an overwhelming upset, Tunney defeated Dempsey in the opening moments of their first championship fight. Now, moments before their rematch, Gene Tunney stood in sharp contrast to the challenger. He was pale, almost shy-looking. He stood still while waiting for the fight to begin.

The fight itself was remarkable from the opening bell. Dempsey was tough and aggressive, while Tunney used finesse and patience to score points. By the seventh round, most in attendance seemed to feel that the champion was ahead. But that didn't stop the challenger.

At the beginning of the round, Dempsey came out charging. He immediately cut the ring in half, and then in half again as he moved Tunney to the ropes. Tunney's eyes widened as Dempsey unloaded a wicked left to the cheek and in an almost simultaneous movement landed a devastating overhand right. Then Tunney's eyes began to cloud, and another downpour of punches began.

The 1927 champion, Gene Tunney.

Tunney went down, and the timekeeper began the count. But Dempsey didn't return to a neutral corner as the rules required. The referee yelled, "Get over where you belong!" but Dempsey still didn't move. Finally his cornermen got through to him and Dempsey raced to a neutral corner. All this had delayed the count by four seconds, however. When the count renewed, Tunney was still foggy, but he was beginning to recover. At the count of nine, he was able to stand. But was it really a count of nine?

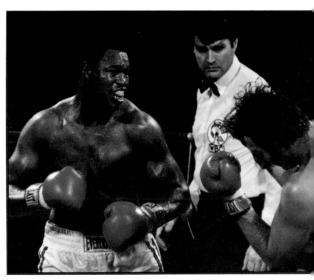

Larry Holmes (left) successfully defends his title against Gerry Cooney in 1982.

Fans around the country were in an uproar; they wanted a rematch. Tunney offered, but Dempsey decided to retire. Dempsey, who was always the perfect gentleman, bowed out graciously. "I had no excuse," he said. "I should have followed the rules. I heard them explained. But let's face it, I came up in a generation when anything went. I had to be ready to protect myself at all times and to take advantage of any situation. Oh, just say a jungle fighter can't change."

THE BROWN BOMBER

The faces of heavyweight boxing changed dramatically in the years following the second Tunney-Dempsey fight. The championship crown was worn by a collection of men—Jack Sharkey, Primo Carnera, Maxie Baer, James J. Braddock—who failed to bring wide recognition to the title. By 1938 many fans were wondering if there would be any more great boxing moments to enjoy. Their question would soon be answered.

Joe Louis, a favorite among boxing fans.

In actuality, including the four-second delay, it had been thirteen seconds since Tunney had been knocked to the canvas. Dempsey had caused the stoppage, but shouldn't he still be champion?

It was not to be. In the eighth round, Tunney regained his strength and found his mind, legs, and fists for the remainder of the fight. At the end of the bout, as the slips were being collected, Dempsey's battered face was testimony to his despair. The decision was unanimous: Tunney remained the champ.

1933 champion Primo Carnera.

It was the late 1930s, a time of tension and political turmoil in the world. Nazi Germany and its leader, Adolf Hitler, had begun their march across Europe. Germans were to be the heart and soul of the "master race," and boxer Max Schmeling was one of Hitler's prime examples. Thus, for many, Schmeling versus a black American named Joe Louis became more than a boxing match; it became a political debate.

Hitler cabled good-luck wishes to Schmeling. United States President Franklin D. Roosevelt encouraged Louis to "beat the German." Yet for the fighters themselves it was something more important— it was a boxing match for the world's heavyweight championship.

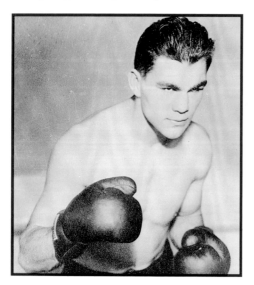

Max Schmeling.

Mike Tyson (left) and Razor Ruddock.

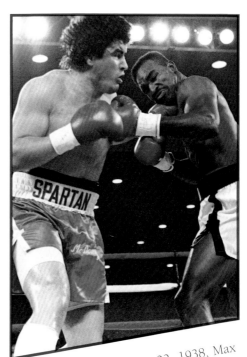

On the evening of June 22, 1938, Max Schmeling walked into a jam-packed Yankee Stadium. As he approached the ring, he was booed and taunted. Spectators pelted him with paper cups, cigarette packs, and even banana peels. Not even the police could stop the fans' violence.

Evander Holyfield (right) faces Seamus McDonough in a 1990 bout.

Several minutes later, the boisterous crowd came to an eerie silence as both fighters were called to the center of the ring. All over America, from Harlem to Hanover, people adjusted their radios. The moment of truth was at hand.

In some last-second instructions, Joe's cornermen warned him of Schmeling's thunderbolt right. Joe remembered how that thunderbolt brought him down in his

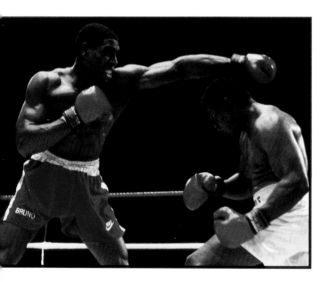

Quick Tillis (right) avoids a jab from Frank Bruno in a 1987 heavyweight match.

first fight with Schmeling, two years earlier. It was the first time Louis had been knocked down. He cried in the dressing room that night. Now he had a score to settle.

The bell rang, and Joe Louis exploded out of his corner. He was a whirlwind of pent-up aggression. Schmeling never knew what hit him: A left jab, a hook to the body, a left hook to Schmeling's cheek that snapped his head back. Schmeling couldn't find any daylight. Louis buried him with punches. Schmeling tried to turn away from the onslaught. A roundhouse right from Louis hammered into Schmel-

Joe Frazier (right), heavyweight champ from 1970 to 1973.

ing's back and cracked two vertebrae. Schmeling screeched in pain. More rights and lefts rained down as Schmeling's knees buckled. The referee waved Louis away and started a standing count. Schmeling pulled away, and Louis attacked the German again. The crowd was in near hysteria as Louis knocked Schmeling down again and again. By the fourth knockdown Schmeling's corner tried to get the fight stopped. Schmeling struggled to get up, but it was all over.

Joe Louis had been a one-man wrecking crew. His 124 seconds of leather-throwing fury had ended the grudge match. In the dressing room after the fight, the reporters tried to get Louis to say he hated Schmeling. Louis just smiled and said, "I'm champ now." "The fight didn't last long," a reporter quipped. "But it was good as long as it lasted," replied Joe.

From coast to coast, thousands of radio listeners celebrated. Joe Louis had united America. "What my father did," his son said later, "was enable white America to think of him as an American, not as black. . . . By winning he became white America's first black hero."

Ezzard Charles (right), the next great champion after Louis, delivers a blow to Jersey Joe Walcott.

Muhammad Ali.

THE GREATEST

Another American hero was the man responsible for perhaps more great moments in heavyweight boxing than any other. Many consider this man one of the greatest athletes of all time. His name became a battle cry: "Ali, Ali, Ali!"

Muhammad Ali was born January 17, 1942, in Louisville, Kentucky. His name at that time was Cassius Marcellus Clay, Jr. The young Clay's remarkable boxing career began eleven years later in a Louisville boys' club. Only six weeks after he started training, Cassius won his first boxing match. It would be the first of many victories.

In a distinguished amateur career that lasted seven years, his numerous wins included two National Golden Gloves titles and concluded with a gold medal triumph in the 1960 Summer Olympics. As a professional his success continued. Clay convincingly won his first several pro fights, and by the age of twenty-two became the Heavyweight Champion of the World by defeating Sonny Liston.

The day after the fight, Cassius made an announcement that would change his life. He indicated that he had become a member of the Muslim religion. He was no longer to be called Cassius Clay. His name was now Cassius X. Four weeks later he would change his name again—to Muhammad Ali. This time it would stick.

1965: Ali knocks out Sonny Liston to retain his title.

Pages 20–21: Mike Tyson (left) combats 1990 challenger Buster Douglas.

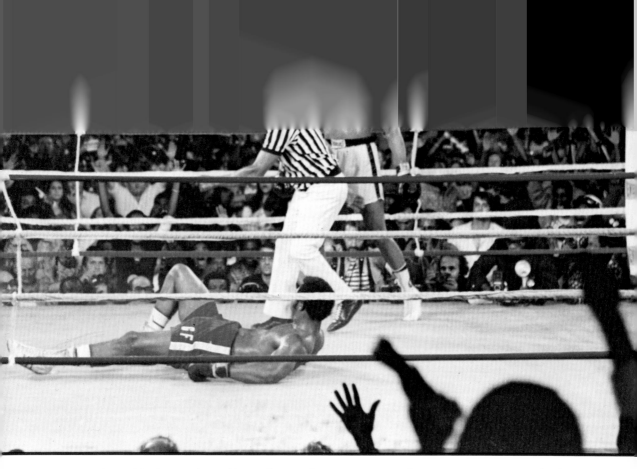

As a Muslim and as Ali, Muhammad became a legend. His boxing greatness continued, but it went beyond that. It had to do with who he was as a person. Gary Smith of *Sports Illustrated* noted, "Ali was a doorway, an opening into something beyond. He spoke of God before his fights, he spoke of man, he spoke of hungry children; he raised the game to drama. And because he stood for something greater, the people who climbed upon their chairs for him felt it: They stood for something greater, too."

On October 1, 1975, more people than ever before were standing for Muhammad Ali. Thousands upon thousands of fight fans had gathered in Manila, the Philippines, to watch Ali do battle. Millions more were watching via closed-circuit television around the world. It had taken four years and two previous fights to build this tension, and now the moment was here. It was Muhammad Ali versus Joe Frazier.

Ali scores a knockout against George Foreman.

These two great fighters had become almost synonymous in their greatness. They had fought two previous times, with each claiming a victory—Frazier in their first bout in 1971 and Ali in the rematch in January of 1974.

Their evenness was one aspect that made the bouts great, but there was another as well. The Ali-Frazier matchups were also extraordinary because of the fighters' conflicting styles. Ali was the smooth, fast-talking boxer. "I float like a butterfly and sting like a bee," quipped the poet Ali. Frazier, on the other hand, was the stern and quiet street fighter. Every battle Frazier fought was a struggle for survival. Their third and final bout was a personification of the individuals.

Ali called the third fight "The Thrilla in Manila." Frazier claimed it was just another fight. Ali antagonized Frazier by calling him ignorant and ugly. Frazier countered by refusing to call Ali by his Muslim name. Instead, he called him "Clay." Beyond the hype, each fighter knew that the bout would be a war.

Frazier and Ali in the 1974 rematch.

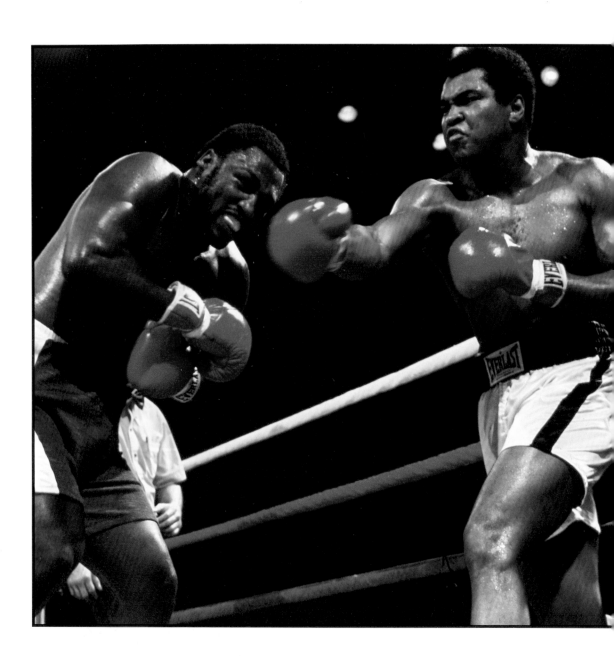

As the opening bell rang, no one knew quite what to expect. Would Ali bob and weave? Would Frazier go for the knockout? Initially there was a surprise. Ali seemed to grow in stature as he approached Frazier. He looked huge as he came to the center of the ring and stood flat-footed, delivering punch after punch to Frazier's head. Ali was not dancing; he was delivering bombs. In fact, Frazier's knees buckled three times in the very first round. "He won't call you Clay no more," screamed Ali's cornerman, Bundini Brown.

A hint of change, however, came in the fourth round. Frazier began steaming back. He began keeping inside of Ali's long reach, delivering short, compact blows to the weary Ali. For the next several rounds, this trend continued. In the sixth, it appeared as though Ali was in trouble. His legs were searching for the floor; only desire to win kept him standing.

Ali hears counsel from Bundini Brown (top) and trainer Angelo Dundee.

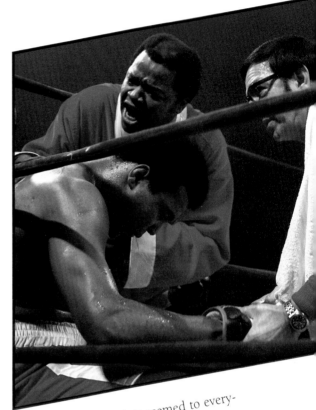

By the tenth round, it seemed to everyone that Frazier had the lead and total command of the fight. Even Ali was concerned. "Old Joe Frazier," he yelled. "Why I thought you were washed up!"

"Somebody told you wrong, pretty boy," Frazier snapped back.

The next round brought a moment that everyone thought for certain was the end. Ali was trapped in Frazier's corner. The fans climbed onto their chairs, screaming in anticipation. But somehow Muhammad escaped. He spun out of the jam and flicked a quick right to Frazier's head. Out of nowhere Ali seemingly had returned.

Several more rapid punches to Frazier's mouth seemed to reinforce this belief. Now blood was beginning to trickle from Joe's mouth. His face was puffy, and his punches were losing strength. "Look at him, he ain't got no power," yelled Ali's trainer Angelo Dundee. Ali began to come at Frazier with every ounce of energy he had left.

Evander Holyfield (left) lands a punch to George Foreman in 1991.

Muhammad Ali.

Joe Frazier.

In the thirteenth round, Ali hit Frazier so hard his mouthpiece flew into the press row. In the fourteenth Ali hit Frazier with nine consecutive right hands. By the end of the round, the referee had to lead "Smokin' Joe" back to his corner.

Holyfield knocks down Buster Douglas to win the title.

Between rounds Frazier's trainer, Eddie Futch, told his fighter that he was going to stop the fight. "No, no Eddie ya can't do that to me," Joe pleaded.

"You couldn't see in the last two rounds," Futch replied.

The Champ.

"I want him, boss," demanded Frazier.

"Sit down, son," said Futch. "It's all over. No one will ever forget what you did here today."

In his hotel room the next day, Ali reflected on the bout. "I was saying to myself, 'Why am I doing this?' You get so tired. It takes so much out of you mentally. It changes you. It makes you a little insane. I was thinkin' at the end, 'What am I doin' here against this beast of a man?' It's so painful, I must be crazy. I always bring out the best in the men I fight, but Joe Frazier, I'll tell the world right now, brings out the best in me. I'm gonna tell you that's one helluva man and God bless him."

THE UNEXPECTED

Engaging personalities like Muhammad Ali have helped make heavyweight boxing one of the most dramatic spectacles in sports. Since the early days of John L. Johnson, thousands of fans have gathered to witness the great moments of a heavyweight bout.

The Mike Tyson–James Douglas fight in Tokyo was no different. Thousands of people were in attendance, and millions of fans around the world had gathered to witness this contest for the 1990 heavyweight championship of the world.

Frank Bruno signals a victory after a 1987 bout.

A day before the fight, the press room was full of bright flashes. Mike Tyson looked inhuman through the strobe effect of the cameras. James "Buster" Douglas stared at the flickering image of his opponent. He was being ignored. Not a single photographer took his picture; he was invisible. Buster was thousands of miles away from his home in Columbus, Ohio —a stranger in a foreign land.

Mike Tyson, the champ, was invincible. He was ready for Douglas. James was another rag doll to be disposed of in the scrap heap along with Spinks, Williams, Bruno, and Holmes. In his five-year career, Tyson had knocked out thirty-three men while winning thirty-seven bouts. Douglas was assumed to be the next.

Mike Tyson (right) in a 1991 contest with Razor Ruddock.

Now, as the referee's count reached seven, the predictions seemed to be coming true. Douglas lay flat on the canvas, unable to move. The fight would soon be over, and Tyson would still be champion.

But at this great moment, something unexpected occurred. Buster Douglas, the forgotten challenger, climbed to his feet at the count of nine. Douglas had dedicated this fight to his mother, who had recently died of a stroke. He was not about to let his dream die on a canvas so far from home.

Seconds later, after the referee had signaled the fighters to begin fighting, Tyson stormed to the middle of the ring. Immediately, Douglas greeted him with a right to the nose. Tyson coiled and tried to throw a left hook, but Douglas hit him with a right to the head. Buster's reach was now frustrating Tyson.

Douglas's corner grew wilder with each succeeding punch. "There ain't no iron in Mike," they yelled. Halfway through the eighth round, Buster hit Tyson with a chopping right hand, and Tyson's left eye began to swell. As a result, Tyson was unable to see many of the challenger's punches.

Tyson goes down.

Buster seized the moment and kept his dream alive. He attacked Iron Mike. He closed Tyson's left eye completely and bullied Tyson into the ropes. Douglas landed four punches that shook Tyson. The punches flopped the champion's head back. Buster Douglas was ten feet tall. Newsrooms around the world were busy sending out the word: Tyson was getting beat.

With one final assault, James Douglas sent Mike Tyson to his end. Douglas pummeled Tyson with lefts and rights until his only escape was down. At the count of nine, with his mouthpiece sticking grotesquely out of his mouth, Tyson was counted out. Nine—ten—ten—ten; the count echoed through the stadium. Mike Tyson, never before knocked down, was not only down but now he was out.

After the fight, Douglas tearfully dedicated the championship to his mother. His eleven-year-old son, Lamar, was hoisted onto his father's shoulders. He was wearing a Buster Douglas hat that read, "Only My Best, James Douglas."

"Only his best" was good enough for James Douglas in one of heavyweight boxing's greatest moments.

A jubilant homecoming for Buster Douglas.